TWELVE THRILLING TALES

TWELVE
THRILLING
TALES

TWELVE THRILLING TALES

RITA CHEMINAIS

Matador
9 Priory Business Park,
Wistow Road, Kibworth Beauchamp,
Leicestershire. LE8 0RX
Tel: 0116 279 2299
Email: books@troubador.co.uk
Web: www.troubador.co.uk/matador
Twitter: @matadorbooks

ISBN 978 1785893 575

British Library Cataloguing in Publication Data.
A catalogue record for this book is available from the British Library.

Printed and bound in the UK by TJ International, Padstow, Cornwall
Typeset in 11pt Aldine401 BT by Troubador Publishing Ltd, Leicester, UK

Matador is an imprint of Troubador Publishing Ltd

For my uncle, Captain Derek Brear, and my tutor, June Davies at Liverpool Rotunda Writers, who gave me the inspiration and encouragement to write this first short story collection.

CONTENTS

DIAMONDS ARE FOREVER

Max and Camilla Partridge had finally sold their jeweller's business. They were both looking forward to enjoying a Mediterranean cruise to celebrate the start of their retirement. As they boarded the *Queen Elizabeth* liner at Southampton they were feeling rather apprehensive, after hearing stormy weather was forecast around the Bay of Biscay. A bellboy directed Max and Camilla to their stateroom, which was located midship (port side) on the high deck.

Max and Camilla began to unpack their suitcases and place their valuables in the stateroom safe. There was a knock at the door, which Max answered. To his utter amazement, standing before him was Gloria Blair – a former assistant, who used to work in their jeweller's store. She was wearing an elegant black cocktail dress and a diamond necklace. In her hand she clutched a diamond-encrusted evening bag.

Max was as white as a sheet, and remained speechless.

This can't possibly be real, Max thought to himself, *because Gloria Blair disappeared five years ago, presumed dead, following a diamond theft at our Partridge's jeweller's store.*

Newspaper reports at the time speculated that Miss Gloria Blair had been kidnapped and subsequently killed by a ruthless diamond thief.

"Well, hello Max," said Gloria. "Fancy seeing you here after all this time. I bet you never imagined I would reappear again after having gone missing, presumed dead."

On hearing Gloria's voice Camilla rushed over to join Max at the stateroom door.

"Hello, Gloria. Max and I, like the police and the press, thought you had been murdered. The stolen diamonds were never recovered, you know. I notice you still have a passion for wearing diamonds, Gloria."

"Well, sorry to disappoint you, Camilla. Here I am. Perhaps you and Max would like to join me after dinner this evening at ten for a drink in the Commodore Club bar… Look forward to catching up."

"OK. S-s-s-see you later," stammered Max, closing the stateroom door quickly.

"Can you believe the coolness of that woman, Max? What a nerve she has got… turning up like this, out of the blue. I sincerely hope she isn't going to ruin our cruise of a lifetime."

Max returned to finish his unpacking. He found it difficult to concentrate on what he was doing. Camilla suggested they open the complimentary bottle of champagne in their room, enjoy their chocolates and watch a film on the television.

"How about watching the James Bond film *Diamonds Are Forever*, or *The Return of the Pink Panther*?" said Camilla.

"I don't think either film would be appropriate to watch, Camilla," remarked Max abruptly.

"I was only joking, my love. Relax, unwind and focus on having a really good time on board ship."

"Do you honestly think it is possible to relax, Camilla, with the return of Gloria Blair? It is almost as if she knew we were going to be on board this ship."

"You're becoming obsessed with the woman, Max. She's only an ex-employee who disappeared five years ago, at the time of the shop break-in and theft. We got most of the money back for the lost diamonds on our business insurance anyway."

"You are probably right, Camilla. As usual. I'm overreacting. I promise I won't give Gloria Blair a second thought from now on. Let's finish the champagne, take an afternoon nap and enjoy a shower together before we dress for dinner," suggested Max.

"Sounds good to me, Max. Let's go for it."

Max and Camilla dressed for dinner. The beautiful diamond necklace Camilla wore glistened and glittered like a million stars lighting up the night sky.

"You look wonderful, darling," whispered Max, as he gently kissed Camilla's neck.

Their table in the Queen's Grill restaurant by the window was perfect, as they could see the white crests of the waves striking the side of the ship as it sailed across the sea. After enjoying a delicious meal and an excellent bottle of Malbec wine they made their way to the Commodore Club bar at the front of the ship.

It was dark outside. Max and Camilla could feel the ship rolling from side to side.

Gloria waved to them as they entered the bar. She beckoned them over to join her for a drink. Max ordered three double amarettos with ice. Gloria opened the conversation after an initial pause of silence.

"Well, isn't this nice? The three of us all together again. How long, Max, did you think you could get away with the theft of the diamonds from your store?"

Max nearly choked on his drink and remarked,

"I don't know what on earth you are talking about, Gloria."

"Oh, come on, Max. Don't act the innocent with me. You've had five good years free from me and the law. Now it's time for you to pay the price for involving me in your little game of fraud and deception. I bet Camilla would love to know what you've really been doing over the last five years. I suggest we all leave the bar now and we continue this discussion outside on deck. I've got a gun in my bag – so don't try any funny business, either of you."

Max and Camilla walked out of the bar ahead of Gloria, who followed close behind them. The ship was really rolling from side to side. They all struggled to walk in a straight line. It was absolute madness to go outside on deck in such stormy weather.

As Max opened the deck door the wind howled and the spray from the sea hit the deck. A ship's officer passed them and suggested it would be unwise to remain on deck in the current weather conditions. Gloria told him they only wanted a quick smoke, and that they would shelter by the deck door. The ship's officer said he would return in ten minutes to check that they had returned to their rooms safely.

Perfect, thought Gloria to herself. *Ten minutes is all I need.*

Camilla clung to Max, not knowing exactly what Gloria was going to do next.

Gloria told them both to move over to the ship's side rail, out of view of the door.

"Don't try to call for help," said Gloria, "otherwise you are both going to pay the price. Give me your necklace, Camilla."

Camilla undid her diamond necklace and passed it over to Gloria. Max made a sudden run to grab Gloria's bag as she was taking the necklace from Camilla's hand. Gloria, however, was too quick for Max, and she fired the gun through her bag.

Max fell to the deck with a thud. Blood began to ooze out on to the front of his shirt where she had shot him in the chest. Camilla screamed.

"Shut up," yelled Gloria." You are going to have to help me push Max over the side of the ship."

Camilla and Gloria pushed Max's body over the side of the ship. Gloria threw her bag into the sea. Gloria turned round and looked at Camilla, and Camilla stared at Gloria. Neither spoke to each other. Just then the deck door opened and the same ship's officer they had met before asked them to return inside.

"Where is the gentleman who was with you before?" enquired the ship's officer.

"Oh, he finished his cigarette earlier than us and he has already returned to his stateroom. We were just about to go back to our rooms too, officer… weren't we, Camilla?"

Camilla didn't reply. The officer said,

"Goodnight, ladies," and locked the deck door behind them as they made their way back to their staterooms.

"Well, Camilla, our little plan worked beautifully. Max hadn't got a clue what was going to happen to him. Let's get a good night's sleep, and in the morning you report your husband missing to the ship's purser. Here, you had better take your diamond necklace back. Diamonds are forever ours. Goodnight, Camilla. Sleep well."

THE BROWN SUGAR CAFE

It was ten o'clock in the morning, and Jason Savage had not turned up for his eight o'clock shift at the Brown Sugar Cafe in Little Wellings. Jan Harvey, manager and owner of the popular retro-style cafe, had been ringing Jason's mobile phone number at regular intervals throughout the morning, but had continued to get no reply.

Jason was never late for work. This was so out of character. Jan could manage to cover the breakfast and morning coffee trade alone, but lunchtime would be a struggle for her on her own.

Jan decided to give Tina, her part-time waitress, a call on her phone to see if she could come in earlier and do the lunchtime shift with her. Tina said she could help out for an hour, from twelve to one. But she had to collect her daughter from nursery at one thirty, and take her to her mum's before returning to do the afternoon tea shift at the cafe. Jan thanked her, but still hoped that Jason would appear before lunchtime.

Steve Pratt, a local builder, and one of Jan's regular customers, came into the cafe carrying a copy of the *Little Wellings Gazette* under his arm.

"Morning, Jan. Can I have the usual, please? Have you seen the headlines on the front page of this morning's *Gazette*?"

"No. I haven't had a minute's break, as Jason hasn't turned up for work yet."

"Well," said Steve, "the police have found an unidentified body floating in the canal by the railway bridge."

"Really?" remarked Jan. "Probably just another bloke who has had too much to drink, lost his balance and accidentally fallen into the canal."

"Let's hope you are right, Jan," remarked Steve. "The police are keen to speak to anyone who may have seen something between nine o'clock last night and six o'clock this morning, when the body was discovered."

As Steve tucked into his full English breakfast Jan asked if she could have a look at the *Gazette*'s front page. She wondered if she should contact the police to report Jason not having turned up for work. Could the body found in the canal be Jason?

Jan thought she was probably worrying unnecessarily. So far Jason was only two hours late. Just then the cafe door opened and in strolled Jason, looking like death warmed up and as white as a sheet.

"What time do you call this, Jason? You look dreadful," remarked Jan.

"Sorry, Jan, I overslept. I was at a friend's party last night, and had a bit too much to drink."

"I've been ringing your mobile all morning, Jason, and getting no response."

"I couldn't find my mobile phone this morning, Jan. I must have left it at my friend's house."

"That must explain why I kept getting no reply," grumbled Jan.

Steve Pratt had finished his breakfast. He decided it was time to get back to work. He paid Jan for his breakfast and left the cafe, deciding it was probably best to leave Jason and Jan to sort out any differences between them. Jason slunk into the kitchen, took off his coat and put on his waiter's apron. Jan shot through to the kitchen.

"Listen, Jason, I've asked Tina to come in at twelve to help out at lunchtime, because I thought you were not going to appear. Are you sure you are fit to work?"

"Yes, I'll be OK, Jan. Ring Tina back and tell her to come in at her usual time for the afternoon shift."

"OK, Jason, I will ring Tina. I'm docking your wages, though, for the time you have been absent from work this morning."

"Fair enough, Jan. I fully understand how you feel about my lateness."

Jan wondered if she was being too hard on Jason. After all, he had never been late for work before. Perhaps she should just give him a warning. However, she was the boss, and he had to learn a lesson about punctuality for work. Jason started to clear the tables from breakfast, wipe them down and lay them up again for lunch.

He asked Pete the chef what the specials were for lunch and promptly wrote them up on the chalkboard in the cafe. Jan watched Jason as he worked, and thought he looked tense and pensive.

The cafe's regulars began to arrive for lunch. Between them Jan and Jason took their orders and served their meals. Jason had got one order muddled up – but otherwise he appeared to be coping well, despite his hangover. By two o'clock Tina had arrived for her afternoon shift. She was pleased to see that Jason and Jan had relaid the tables for afternoon tea. Tina looked at Jason and remarked jokingly,

"My God, Jason, you look rough. Were you out on the ale last night? That's not like you. Don't put the customers off their afternoon tea." Jason gave Tina a withering look, and went back into the kitchen for some more glasses.

Just at that moment the cafe door opened and in walked two smartly dressed men in suits. One of them showed Jan his ID card and said, "We are looking for a young man called Jason Savage. We have reason to believe he works here."

Jan was taken by surprise, and thought to herself,

Why are these two plain-clothed police detectives keen to find Jason? Jan responded to the detective's enquiry.

"Yes, Jason Savage does work here. He's just popped into the kitchen for some glasses. I'll go and get him for you now."

"Thank you. That would be helpful, Miss."

"Oh, I'm Jan Harvey, owner and manager of the Brown Sugar Cafe. I won't be a minute." Jan walked into the kitchen.

"Hey Jason, there are two police detectives in the cafe. They would like to speak to you."

As Jason turned to face Jan he accidentally knocked a couple of glasses off the tray. They smashed as they hit the ground.

"I'm sorry, Jan. I'll pay for the breakage. Let me clear the mess up."

"No, Jason. You go out and talk to those two detectives before the customers begin to arrive for afternoon tea. I'll clear up the broken glass."

Jason walked out of the kitchen. He was immediately greeted by one of the detectives.

"Are you Jason Savage?"

"Yes, I am."

"We would be grateful if you would accompany us to the police station… to help us with our enquiries regarding an incident involving a man found dead early this morning in the canal."

"I don't know anything about a body found in the canal. I was at home late last night, sleeping off a hangover," insisted Jason.

"Get your coat, Jason. We will continue this conversation down at the station."

Jan and Tina stared at Jason open-mouthed as he went to get his coat.

"You can manage without him, can't you, Miss?" asked one of the detectives.

"Yes. Tina and I will manage without him this afternoon."

They both watched from the cafe window as Jason was escorted to a dark blue Ford Mondeo by the two police detectives.

That was the very last time Jan and Tina saw Jason Savage. He never returned to work, and they never heard anything back from the police.

Three days later Jan picked up the morning edition of the *Little Wellings Gazette* as it landed with a thud on the floor after dropping through the cafe's letter box. The front-page news reported that Jason Savage was actually Benny Doyle, a known identity fraudster who had been wanted by the police. Benny Doyle had been blackmailing and harassing the real Jason Savage. He had taken his passport, his National Insurance documents and a considerable amount of cash from Jason's flat. The motive for the crime was that Jason had gone off with Benny's long-term girlfriend.

After considerable police questioning Benny Doyle had confessed to the murder of Jason Savage. Benny had got involved in a fight with Jason on his way back from a party. Benny had pushed Jason deliberately into the canal. Jason couldn't swim. Benny panicked and ran away from the canal. In his haste to leave the scene of the crime Benny's mobile phone had dropped out of his pocket on to the canal path.

As Jan was putting up an advertisement for a new waiter in the window of the Brown Sugar Cafe she thought to herself how stupid she had been to be fooled so easily by Jason's – or, rather, Benny's deception. He had seemed such a quiet nice young man, who had kept himself to himself. She never dreamt he wasn't who he said he was.

However, Jan never really knew anything about Benny's life outside work.

Better luck next time, she said to herself, *with the appointment of a new full-time waiter.* She would be sure to check their identity and paperwork very carefully. Despite the scandal, business at the cafe was booming even more than usual.

The Brown Sugar Cafe nearly turned into Black Treacle, with all the excitement of the local crime incident.

THE MURDER MYSTERY
WEEKEND FROM HELL

P ete and Anne were good companions. They fancied
a weekend experience with a difference. Pete booked
a murder mystery weekend at the Old Swan Hotel in
Harrogate. The scenario was a country house gathering
of family and friends to celebrate a birthday.

Pete and Anne arrived at the Old Swan Hotel to check
in for two o'clock on Saturday afternoon. They went up
to their room, unpacked and made their way downstairs
to the lounge for afternoon tea at three o'clock. This
was the first part of the murder mystery experience.
Pete and Anne mingled with the other guests, some of
whom were actors. They began to listen and look out for
clues. Anne had a small notepad and pen in her handbag.
When she or Pete thought they had discovered a strong
clue Anne made a note of it for later reference.

"This is fabulous, Pete," remarked Anne
enthusiastically, as she tucked into her afternoon tea.

"Good. Have you spotted who the actors are yet,
Anne?"

"I think I've identified two or three of them. Did you
observe anything, Pete, when you scanned the lounge?"

"I noticed that the old chap sitting by the bar passed

a note to a tall young man wearing a bright blue jumper. Don't know whether that's significant… "

"Well, I'll jot it down, Pete."

The murder mystery weekend coordinator, Dan Johnson, suddenly appeared in the lounge.

"Good afternoon, ladies and gentlemen. You are welcome to go off now and enjoy some free time in Harrogate. We meet again tonight in the Library restaurant at seven thirty sharp for dinner. It will be formal dress."

Pete and Anne walked in the Valley Gardens. On their way back to the hotel they went into the art gallery. Pete spotted the tall young man in the bright blue jumper.

"Oh, look, Anne. It's that young man I saw in the lounge at the hotel taking the note from the old chap at the bar. Shall I ask him what was in the note, just in case it's a vital clue?"

"If you really must, Pete." Pete went over to the tall young man.

"Excuse me… I saw you earlier at the afternoon tea at the Old Swan Hotel. I don't know if there was anything relevant written in the note that the old chap at the bar passed to you, was there?"

The young man turned around to face Pete and replied, "I'm not at liberty to discuss any action you may have observed earlier with you now."

Anne apologised.

"Sorry. Pete thinks he's Hercule Poirot, and does have a tendency to take his powers of detection too far."

"No worries. See you later this evening."

The tall young man walked quickly to the exit of the art gallery, where he promptly made a call on his mobile phone. He appeared rather agitated.

"I wonder who he was speaking to, Pete," remarked Anne inquisitively.

"I don't know, my love. Let's make our way back to the hotel."

"OK, Hercule," joked Anne.

Pete and Anne made their way downstairs to the Library restaurant. They were shown to their places at the dinner table by Dan Johnson. Pete sat next to the old chap he had seen at the lounge bar during afternoon tea. Anne was sitting next to a blonde-haired woman in a skimpy black dress. When Dan Johnson introduced the main murder mystery characters it turned out that the old chap was Lord Haversham and the young blonde was Susie Manning – girlfriend of Ralph Haversham, the youngest son, who just happened to be the tall young man.

As the dinner progressed and the wine flowed endlessly the conversation became more animated between the guests and the actors. Pete was like Hawkeye, never missing a move, or an aside, from any of the murder mystery characters.

Anne thought the maid who was waiting at table resembled someone she knew.

Just at that moment Pete slumped face first into his dessert. Everyone stopped eating and turned towards Pete. Anne gave Pete a nudge, but he didn't stir.

"Oh, my God," said Anne. "What has happened to my boyfriend? He can't be dead... surely not?"

The maid waiting at table dropped the empty dessert plates she was carrying. One of the waiters rushed to help her rescue the fragments of crockery strewn across the carpet. Ralph Haversham got up and left the room.

Dan Johnson was mortified. He asked everyone to go to the Library bar. Anne insisted on staying with Pete until the police, the doctor and the paramedics arrived.

"This wasn't supposed to happen," explained Dan Johnson to the diners. "Lord Haversham was to be the murder victim. I must ask you all to remain here, as the police will want to ask you some questions about the evening's events."

Anne was still sitting next to Pete in the Library restaurant. She was traumatised by what had happened. Anne suddenly remembered who the maid waiting at table reminded her of. It was a long-lost acquaintance called Rachel. Of course... Anne had heard she was working as a film extra. Perhaps she might know something. If only she could catch Rachel's attention and speak to her. This had turned into the weekend from hell for Anne.

Anne was moved to a smaller, private lounge. Close examination of Pete's body by the doctor and the police inspector revealed the cause of death as poisoning.

Pete's body was taken away to the police mortuary. Witness statements were taken from all present, including Anne. The hotel and grounds were searched extensively for the missing actor, Ralph Haversham. He wasn't found.

When Anne eventually returned home and entered her house Rachel and the tall young man who played Ralph Haversham were sitting before her in the lounge.

"Hello, Anne. We thought you wouldn't want to return to an empty house... So sorry your twit of a boyfriend got Lord Haversham's poison by mistake. He really was becoming a threat, going on about the note," remarked Rachel.

The tall young man pointed a gun at Anne.

"We can't let you live, either. Goodbye Anne." He shot Anne. She fell down on to the lounge floor. After taking Anne's notepad from her bag and removing all traces of fingerprints – and the gun – Rachel and the tall young man vacated the house via the back door.

"Phew! Those amateur sleuths nearly blew our cover. If they had found out what was written on that note we would both be doing time now at Her Majesty's pleasure," remarked Rachel.

The note written by the old chap at the bar, which he handed to the young tall man, had said,

I'm watching you and your girlfriend, who is playing the maid. I should have informed the police a year ago about how you murdered that wealthy old lady at Sunnyside Mansions.

Don't let history repeat itself tonight.

GARDEN MAKEOVER

Fred and Nora Bates looked out of the window of their bungalow onto their rain-sodden garden.

"Not ideal weather for the start of our garden makeover, Nora," exclaimed Fred, a retired escapologist.

"No, indeed it isn't," replied Nora.

At that moment two large transit vans pulled up outside the front of Fred and Nora's home. Written across the side of each van was *CREATIVE GARDEN ANGELS*.

"My goodness," remarked Fred, "I didn't imagine the garden makeover we won in the magazine competition would be such a big job."

"It will certainly give the neighbours something to look at over the next few days," said Nora.

The front doorbell rang. Fred went to answer it. Standing before him was the most gorgeous garden angel he had ever seen. She looked like a Pre-Raphaelite goddess.

"Good morning. I'm Jasmine Hollis, from Creative Garden Angels. You must be Fred and Nora Bates."

"That's correct," replied Fred, mesmerised by the delightful young red-haired beauty standing before him.

"May I come in and share the provisional plans for the garden makeover with you both before the groundworks team make a start?" asked Jasmine.

Fred, Nora and Jasmine viewed and discussed the provisional plans for the garden makeover. There was a unanimous agreement about the location of the pond, with its impressive water feature. This was to be located in a corner of the back garden. Jasmine explained to Fred and Nora that a small excavator would be used to dig the eight foot long by three foot deep hole for the pond liner. The earth removed from the pond site would create the raised flower beds in the front garden. The project would be completed within four days, irrespective of the weather.

Work commenced on the preparation of the garden's main areas for redesign and redevelopment. Creating the pond with the water feature was the largest aspect of the garden makeover project.

The small excavator made its way into the back garden. It was driven by a surly-looking giant of a labourer. He had been subcontracted by Jasmine. He wasn't a full-time member of the groundworks team.

Fred and Nora kept an eye on progress from the bungalow windows. The team of six groundworkers, which included Jasmine, appeared to work efficiently together.

Nora kept the gardeners supplied with hot drinks and biscuits throughout the day. Fred was considered to be very lucky to have such a treasure of a wife as Nora.

The nosy gardening neighbour from hell, John Partridge, regarded himself as the Alan Titchmarsh of Winkleton.

He kept an equally close eye on the work from over his garden fence. He couldn't resist trying to disrupt the work of the Creative Garden Angels with his unhelpful comments about how they should be doing the garden makeover.

Jasmine Hollis just about managed to keep her patience while remaining polite towards the interfering busybody and know-it-all. John Partridge, who had entered the same gardening competition as Nora and Fred, felt very aggrieved that he hadn't won it.

Day two of the garden project saw an improvement in the weather. The pond area was still waterlogged. Therefore the day was spent landscaping the gardens and planting out new shrubs.

"I'm a bit disappointed that work on the pond has stopped," remarked Fred to Jasmine.

"Don't worry, Fred. The team will focus their efforts on the pond construction tomorrow," replied Jasmine.

The remodelled garden was really beginning to take shape. Fred took a walk over to the pond site before bedtime to check if the area was less waterlogged.

The light from the full moon was sufficient for Fred to see by. Just as Fred leant forward to peer down into the deep hole he felt an almighty blow strike the back of his head. He went dizzy. He fell head first into the pond pit, and lost consciousness.

Some time later, when Fred regained consciousness, he felt an overwhelming dampness from the earth on top of him. It was pitch black. Soil was up his nose, and in his eyes, ears and mouth. He felt the unbearable, heavy weight of the damp soil on top of him crushing his ribs and pressing on the sides of his head like a vice.

Fred tried to move his arms and get his hands free. It was no good. The weight of the wet earth was defeating him. Despite Fred having previously been an escapologist, he suffered from taphephobia – the fear of being buried alive in the ground. It was no use Fred panicking, as he knew that the more he struggled the greater would be the damage to his body. His bones would break, his eyeballs would pop out of their sockets, and he would suffer brain damage.

"Please don't let me die all alone in the darkness," choked Fred, as he lay still and frightened. No one came. No one heard Fred.

The next morning, when the Creative Garden Angels arrived on day three, they were surprised to get no reply when they rang the front doorbell. Jasmine went around to the back and knocked on the kitchen door. Her knock remained unanswered.

Jasmine thought it most unusual that Fred and Nora were not in. Perhaps they had gone out somewhere and had forgotten to tell her.

Never mind. The team will make a start on creating the pond, she decided.

The pond liner was brought across the lawn and laid down at the edge of the hole. The hosepipe was connected to the external water tap in preparation for filling the pond with cold water once the pond liner was secured. Jasmine peered over into the three foot deep hole that had been dug out. To her amazement, she saw a mound of earth lying at the bottom.

How did that get there? she wondered. Jasmine wasn't very impressed with the work of the subcontracted labourer. She called two of her groundworkers over and asked them to shovel out the earth. Within three minutes of them starting to dig they called Jasmine over. To her horror, the body of Fred Bates lay there motionless in the bottom of the pond pit.

"Oh, my God. Is he dead?" enquired Jasmine.

"Yes, I'm afraid he is," replied one of the groundworkers. "I'll telephone the police."

"Leave the body exactly where it is," said Jasmine.

Twenty minutes later a police car arrived outside the bungalow. A forensic team followed closely behind. John Partridge, the neighbour, had spotted the police. He rushed out to his back garden fence and asked what was going on.

"Nothing to concern you, sir. Please go back inside," requested Detective Inspector James.

The forensic team and the police doctor got on with examining the body. The doctor confirmed, with the inspector, that the deceased had received a blow to the back of his head – which was most likely to have been done with a heavy metal implement, such as a garden spade. The blow to the head would have caused the deceased to lose consciousness. In turn, he would have suffocated and died under the weight of the wet earth.

Further examination of the body, back at the mortuary, would provide more conclusive information about the exact cause and time of death.

"It doesn't look good. We have a murder enquiry on our hands," remarked Detective Inspector James. Statements were taken by the police from Jasmine, and from the groundworks team. The hired labourer who operated the excavator would also be questioned later, with the neighbours. The police knocked at the back and front doors of the Bates's bungalow, but got no reply.

"We will come back later on to speak to Mrs Bates. In the meantime, I would request that the garden makeover ceases. The garden is now being treated as a crime scene. It will be sealed off immediately," instructed Detective Inspector James.

Creative Garden Angels packed up their equipment and vacated the garden.

A police search was launched for Nora Bates, who had failed to return to the bungalow. The operator of the excavator was also missing. Local gossip in the neighbourhood was rife, as John Partridge took great delight in spreading nasty rumours about the demise of Fred Bates. Creative Garden Angels moved on to another project.

A month later the *Winkleton Herald* reported that the police had unearthed further evidence to prove that Jim Grimes, the excavator operator, had murdered Fred Bates. Nora Bates was an accessory to the crime. Both were still at large.

An international manhunt was now under way. The motive for the crime was still unknown. However, it had come to light that Jim Grimes had briefly been an escapologist, and an ex-boyfriend of Nora Bates.

DOUBLE DEAL IN NICE

Neville Kent, senior property representative – who works for Graham Chase, managing director and owner of Kent Chase International Properties, based in Knightsbridge, London – is feeling fed up. Graham Chase enters the office looking pleased with himself.

"Good morning. What's making you look sorry for yourself, Neville, on such a beautiful sunny morning?"

"Morning, Graham. I didn't realise I looked so glum. I was thinking about Leoni. How, over the last month, she's been going out for long, lazy lunches with her female friends and shopping until she drops at Harrods and Fortnum and Mason's. When she gets home she is too exhausted to cook the evening meal, and we end up getting a takeaway meal."

"That doesn't sound like my daughter Leoni's usual behaviour," remarked Graham.

"I wonder if the magic is beginning to vanish from our marriage. It's been ages since Leoni and I went away together," muttered Neville.

"Why don't you take Leoni to Nice for a few days this week to rekindle your romance? It's quiet in the office at present."

"That's a wonderful suggestion, Graham. I'll get on with booking our flights and hotel now, if that's OK with you?"

"Of course it is, and enjoy yourselves."

As Leoni finished the last of the packing for the surprise Nice trip with Neville she gave Pierre Le Roi a quick call on her mobile phone.

"Hello, Pierre, my love. I haven't got long to chat. Absolute disaster is about to happen. Neville's booked a three-day break in Nice. It's supposed to be rekindling our sham of a marriage! How are we going to be able to carry out the plan for that property deal you mentioned in Nice with Neville around?"

"Oh, don't worry, my *chérie*. You just need to slip away from Neville for a couple of hours on Wednesday morning to meet the prospective buyer of the apartment. Just tell Neville you want to do some shopping that morning in the designer stores in Nice. We'll agree the final arrangements this Tuesday afternoon."

"OK, Pierre. Love you."

Neville and Leoni's flight left on time from London City Airport. As the plane began its descent into Nice Airport they marvelled at the beautiful azure blue Mediterranean Sea, the wonderful golden beaches and the magnificent luxury boats moored in Nice harbour.

"I'm so glad we are taking this break, Leoni. It will do us both the world of good."

"Let's hope you're right, Neville. I can't wait to shop in the chic Nice boutiques and relax on the golden beach."

After a short taxi ride from the airport they were checked into the Negresco Hotel on the Promenade des Anglais. They were shown to their Napoleon Suite on the second floor. The view from their balcony was to die for, as they looked across to the beach and the inviting blue Mediterranean Sea.

Neville and Leoni unpacked. Neville went to the hotel bar for a couple of drinks and a light snack. Leoni took herself across the road to the Negresco's private Neptune Beach to relax in the sun. Once settled, Leoni rang Pierre on her mobile phone.

"Hi, sweetie. I've arrived in Nice, and I'm relaxing alone on the Neptune beach."

"Listen, Leoni, don't get too relaxed. I've rented some office space to do the apartment sale with the client I've found. Get yourself to 101 Rue du Congrès at ten thirty Wednesday morning. Remember to refer to me as Mr Dupont. Wear something sexy and chic. Look busy at the office desk. Shuffle some papers. Greet the client. He's called Dimitry Yolkin."

"Oh, my God! Is he a Russian oligarch, by any chance, Pierre?"

"Yes. He's something big in oil. I've got a set of keys cut for the apartment. I will have shown Mr Yolkin around the apartment by ten fifteen in the morning. He's already seen the property details in the phoney brochure I got printed, and likes what he's read. We should return to the office by ten forty. The deal will be quick. You will take the deposit of one million euros from him. Be sure to bank that offshore in a few days, when we can split the difference."

"Perfect, Pierre. Neville plans to visit the Matisse Museum tomorrow morning. He's happy for me to shop while he enjoys some culture."

Neville and Leoni, after enjoying a wonderful evening meal in the Rotunda Restaurant at the Negresco Hotel, decided upon an early night, where they rekindled their romance. The next day, after breakfast in their suite, Neville kissed Leoni and wished her well with her morning's shopping. He thought she was rather overdressed. Leoni insisted that she had to look her best when visiting chic French designer dress stores. Neville agreed, and took himself off to the Matisse Museum. They arranged to meet for lunch at the Neptune Beach bar at one in the afternoon.

Leoni made her way to the rented office. She was shown to a desk with a computer near the window. Pierre had left a pile of papers in the in tray, along with some property brochures.

At ten forty Pierre (posing as Mr Dupont, an international property representative from the fictitious Majestic Properties), introduced Leoni as his secretary, Miss LaConte, to Mr Dimitry Yolkin. Once the introductions were over Mr Yolkin paid a deposit of one million euros. Leoni promptly took the deposit and issued a fake receipt from Majestic Properties, signed by Claude Dupont (alias Pierre Le Roi).

Once Mr Yolkin had left the office Pierre helped Leoni clear the desk. They left separately. Leoni carried the briefcase containing the deposit for the apartment back to the Negresco Hotel. She went straight up to her suite, changed into something less formal and promptly left the hotel with the briefcase of money to meet up with Alexei Gavrikov, the real Russian owner of the apartment that Pierre had just sold to Dimitry Yolkin.

Alexei stood up to greet Leoni. Dimitry Yolkin smiled at her and took the briefcase from Leoni. They sat down. Dimitry handed over two cheques, each for a million euros: one for Alexei and the other for Leoni. Dimitry and Alexei had a brief conversation in Russian. Dimitry left the cafe bar. Alexei leant over the table and kissed Leoni longingly on the lips.

"Well, Leoni darling… that should teach Mr Claude Dupont – or should I say Pierre Le Roi? – a lesson on how not to tangle with Russians over a fraudulent property deal. You and I have gained from this situation, while Pierre Le Roi ends up with nothing.

"He has been hoisted by his own petard. I sold the apartment on to another colleague for four million euros, making a nice profit of two million euros.

"See you in Dubai, Leoni, in a month's time, when you have got rid of that wimp of a husband of yours. Take care, Leoni. Oh, and by the way, do give my regards to your father!"

TURMOIL AT THE
BLUE MOON RESTAURANT

F rank and Laura Evans were looking forward to celebrating their fifth wedding anniversary at the Blue Moon restaurant in Chinatown. They didn't dine out together very often: only once in a blue moon, for a special occasion.

As they made their way to the restaurant on this cold October Halloween evening they both marvelled at the sight of the full moon up in the night sky casting its blue rays down on them. Laura shuddered as she heard the howl of a hound in the distance. Frank, being superstitious, turned over a coin in his trouser pocket for good luck.

Mixed emotions hit Frank and Laura.

"Gosh, Frank. It's almost as if the lunar power of the blue moon is creating a mysterious atmosphere this evening."

"I have an uneasy feeling about tonight, Laura. Let's hope the Chinese meal is worth waiting for at the illustrious Blue Moon restaurant."

As Frank and Laura entered the restaurant they were greeted by the manager. He took their coats, showed them to their table and left two menus for them to peruse.

The Chinese music playing softly in the background and the low lights made for a romantic, serene atmosphere. Laura looked around the restaurant. It was comfortably full. A party of four young men, tucking hungrily into their Chinese banquet, caught Laura's attention.

"Hey, Frank... those four young men, who are dressed all in black with blood-red lips and white ghostly faces, look strange. I heard one of them asking the waiter if he was certain that there was no garlic in their food."

"Perhaps they are a group of vampires," joked Frank. "I believe that when there is a blue moon vampires revert back to a human state, free from bloodsucking."

"Oh, don't give me that supernatural baloney, Frank. At least everyone else in the restaurant tonight looks normal, especially that Chinese couple in the corner."

"I wonder if the older Chinese bloke with the young Chinese woman is her sugar daddy," remarked Frank.

"No," replied Laura. "It's obviously father and daughter. You can see the family resemblance."

Frank and Laura ordered their food and a bottle of champagne on ice.

"This is lovely, Frank. Wonderful Chinese food washed down with a fine champagne. What more could a girl ask for?"

"Happy fifth wedding anniversary, Laura."

"Cheers, Frank. And the same to you, my love."

Laura glanced over to the corner table and noticed the older Chinese gentleman making his way to the Gents toilet. He was gone for some time. The young Chinese woman looked anxious.

Just at that moment the restaurant door opened. Two men entered, dressed in black and wearing face masks. The restaurant manager, who was looking troubled, asked them,

"How can I help you? Are you looking for someone?"

The two men ignored him and made their way over to where the young Chinese woman was sitting alone at the table. One of the men took a knife out of his jacket pocket and held it to the throat of the young Chinese woman. She screamed. Everyone in the restaurant looked on, aghast. A sudden disturbance and commotion occurred as the other man in black tied the hands and gagged the mouth of the young Chinese woman.

One of the masked men said to the customers and restaurant staff,

"Everyone stay where you are. No one is to attempt to call the police. If any of you do so you too will be taken away with the Chinese woman."

Frank and Laura looked on in terror. Frank turned a coin over in his trouser pocket for good luck. An atmosphere of fear, unrest and disbelief existed in the restaurant. No one spoke or moved. The two men in black led the young Chinese woman out of the restaurant and into a waiting car. The black Mercedes promptly screeched and sped away at high speed.

The father of the young Chinese woman reappeared in the restaurant. On noticing his daughter was missing he remarked to the restaurant manager, "Where is my daughter?"

The restaurant manager replied, "Your daughter

has just been bound and gagged and taken away by two masked men."

The elderly Chinese gentleman picked up a letter from his table. He opened it. His hands shook as he read the letter. He turned to the restaurant manager and cried out, "My daughter has been kidnapped. Her kidnappers want £1,000,000 pounds. I don't know why she has been taken. I don't have the money to pay for her release. What am I going to do?"

Frank got up from his table and walked over to the Chinese gentleman.

"You are going to have to call the police and report this incident."

"I can't," replied the elderly Chinese gentleman. "I am a Chinese diplomat. My credibility will be compromised. Please, all of you, just go home. There is nothing anyone can do."

Frank returned to his table. He helped Laura on with her coat and paid the bill. Other diners followed suit. Once outside the restaurant Frank and Laura shuddered. They walked away arm in arm in the cold, blue night air. The full moon shone brightly in the night sky, and a hound howled in the distance.

"Well, Laura, that was certainly a night to remember."

"Yes. Thank goodness we only eat out once in a blue moon, Frank."

"I'm so sorry it's spoilt our anniversary celebrations, Laura. Next year we will celebrate our sixth wedding anniversary at home, with a takeaway meal."

Frank and Laura didn't sleep well that night. They spent

it tossing and turning, wondering if the young Chinese woman was still alive.

Over breakfast the next morning Frank and Laura heard the local news briefing on the radio. It announced,

At ten o'clock last night, at the Blue Moon restaurant in Chinatown, a young Chinese woman – Shu Lee Wong, daughter of the Chinese diplomat Chen Lee Wong – was kidnapped by two armed masked men. A ransom of £1,000,000 has been requested by the kidnappers. Chen Lee Wong is helping the police with their enquiries.

A trained negotiator has been commissioned to assist the police in securing the safe return of Shu Lee Wong. The police believe the motive for the kidnapping is that her father, Chen Lee Wong, owes a considerable amount of money – in the form of gambling debts accrued from playing mah-jong. Consequently the Blue Moon restaurant has been temporarily closed by the police, upon discovering an illegal gambling club in the basement of the restaurant.

"Ah," said Frank, "that accounts for why the young Chinese woman's father left their table for some time last night. He must have been trying to win back some –or all – of his lost money in a game of mah-jong in the restaurant's illegal basement gambling club."

"I said to you last night, Frank," remarked Laura, "that the power of the blue moon had created a mysterious atmosphere, casting its omen of bad luck. Looks as if I was right after all."

ONE OF THOSE NIGHTS AT
THE HOTEL CALIFORNIA

The 'Eagle' had landed. Tay Alan, hired assassin, walked over to the bar at the Hotel California. Heads turned to admire the good-looker.

"What can I get you?" said the barman.

"A tequila sunrise with ice would be just perfect."

As Tay Alan got out some cash to pay for the drink a photograph of a young man fell out on to the bar counter. The barman glanced at the photograph.

"Have you seen this guy recently?" enquired Tay Alan.

"No, not recently, but he does drink here on occasions," replied the barman.

Tay Alan slipped the barman a twenty dollar note.

"Let me know when he next appears. I'd like a word with him."

"Will do," replied the barman.

It was Friday the thirteenth. Unlucky for some, but not for Tay Alan, whose horoscope foretold:

Hitting a lucky seam on Friday the thirteenth enables you to take several steps forward in following your intuitive hunch to make a significant move. This will lead to an all-important breakthrough, with you calling the shots, to reach the goal within your grasp.

Tay Alan fancied a bit of 'afternoon delight' before the evening kicked in. However, on looking around the bar, no one appealed enough for Tay to want to fulfil that desire. After leaving the bar Tay Alan moved outside to the poolside and admired the lithe, tanned bodies of the lazy sunbathers. Nothing special there, either. Just the rich and famous enjoying the American dream… while it lasted.

Suddenly, at that moment, Tay Alan's mobile phone rang. On pressing the answer button Tay immediately heard the gruff voice of Frankie Owen, former big time war hero (and now a small fry private eye) asking for an update on progress.

"Not a lot of action here at present," said Tay Alan. "Got the barman on the lookout for the target. Will let you know once the mission is accomplished."

Tay Alan strolled over to an empty table near the poolside and sat down. After taking out a cigarette and lighting up Tay Alan surveyed those swimming in the crystal-clear pool. One guy, who was wearing a pair of tight red Speedos, was of particular interest to Tay.

It can't be? Surely not? It is the assassin's target, marvelled Tay. This assignment was certainly looking like an easy kill – providing Tay could get the target on his own, away from the glitzy crowd.

The target, Monty Scott – desperado, and the most wanted international drug baron – was still enjoying his afternoon swim in the hotel pool. As he swam over to the side of the pool where Tay was sitting he shouted to Tay, "Hey! Could you pass me a towel?"

Tay did as requested.

"Thanks," spluttered Monty Scott as he rubbed himself down with the towel.

"What's the food like in the restaurant?" enquired Tay Alan.

"I've heard it's pretty good. Maybe see you later for a drink?" remarked Monty Scott.

"Maybe," replied Tay Alan.

When Tay eventually got back to the hotel room there was a note pushed under the door. On opening the note Tay read,

> *TONIGHT'S THE NIGHT.*
> *DON'T FORGET THE DUTY-FREE.*
> *SEE YOU AT EIGHT THIS SUNDAY FOR*
> *DINNER.*

Tay took a shower, changed for dinner and transferred the lighter and cigarettes to the jacket hanging over the back of the desk chair.

After dinner in the hotel restaurant Tay strolled through to the hotel bar and sat down at a table. Sitting at the bar was none other than Monty Scott. Tay Alan noticed the barman looking closely at Monty Scott as he took his drinks order. Tay got up from the table and sat on the bar stool next to Monty Scott.

"Hi, there. How are you doing? Let me buy you a drink," said Monty Scott.

"I'm doing fine, thanks. I'd like a tequila sunrise with ice, please," replied Tay Alan.

"I was supposed to be meeting my brother here tonight but for some reason, at the last minute, he couldn't make it," remarked Monty Scott.

"Oh… I'm sorry to hear that," said Tay Alan.

"Listen, it's a lovely warm moonlit night tonight. Why don't we continue our conversation outside, on the poolside terrace? Hey, barman, can you bring the drinks outside?" requested Monty Scott.

Tay Alan and Monty Scott both made their way outside to sit at a table on the terrace. There were no other guests sitting outside. Tay offered Monty Scott a cigarette, which he accepted. Monty Scott leant forward to accept a light from Tay. Tay Alan discreetly pressed the hidden button on the base of the cigarette lighter. This promptly released a shot, which directly hit Monty Scott right between the eyes. He slumped forward, his head hitting the table top.

Tay got up. There was no time to spare. After walking over to the other side of the swimming pool Tay walked out of the open side gate, started up the getaway car, and drove out of the Hotel California. Los Angeles Airport was a thirty-minute drive.

On arrival at the airport Tay Alan checked in and proceeded through security.

After purchasing a couple of items in the duty-free shop Tay went to relax in the airport lounge. Sky News was on the big screen television. Tay Alan glanced at the subtitles as they flashed across the screen. One subtitle of interest reported that Jerry Scott, a Los Angeles city banker – *and identical twin brother of Monty Scott, desperado and international drug baron* – had been found dead on the terrace at the Hotel California. The death was being treated as suspicious.

Tay Alan sat motionless. Friday the thirteenth was certainly one of those nights Tay would never forget. Failing to know that Monty Scott had an identical twin brother was definitely a major oversight on the part of the British intelligence service.

How was Tay Alan, hired assassin, ever going to live this mistake down? More to the point, Monty Scott, the desperado drug baron, was still at large somewhere in the USA. Tay Alan had failed miserably in completing the assignment. This would inevitably result in a permanent foreign posting to some godforsaken outback.

What made the situation so much worse for Tay Alan was the fact that her career – as the only female hired assassin working with British intelligence – was well and truly over. Right now, Tay Alan would welcome a cushy little administrative job in the City of London.

As the London Heathrow flight was called Tay Alan walked casually over to the boarding gate.

A BIRTHDAY TO REMEMBER

Amy was looking forward to celebrating her birthday in London with her good friend Jenny. They travelled down together on the train from up north. The weather was looking good, which pleased Jenny and Amy. The two friends checked into their hotel and unpacked their suitcases. They left the hotel to take the tube to Hyde Park Corner. Jenny hired two bicycles, as she had planned for them to cycle the circuit of Hyde Park. Amy hadn't been on a bicycle for a very long time. She wheeled the bicycle over to the handrail and propped the bicycle against it while she sat herself on the saddle.

Jenny was already cycling ahead, unaware that Amy hadn't even got going yet. Amy started to pedal her bicycle slowly. The bicycle wobbled and off she fell. The bicycle landed on top of her. Amy shouted out to Jenny,

"Wait for me." Jenny looked back in despair, and said, "Hurry up, Amy. What is the problem?"

"Where do I begin?" said Amy. "I can't hold the bicycle upright because it's too heavy."

Eventually, after five more minutes, Amy got the bicycle away from the handrail and began to ride. She started to pick up speed and catch Jenny up.

"How far and for how long are you intending to ride in the park?" enquired Amy?

"I intend to ride around the entire perimeter of the park," replied Jenny.

"Well, I don't think I will be able to do that," remarked Amy.

"Just do your best," said Jenny.

Amy wasn't enjoying the bicycle ride. Her heart was pounding in her chest. She felt very hot and sweaty. Amy pulled over to the handrail in order to take a short rest. Jenny was getting well ahead again, unaware that Amy had stopped cycling. A lady passing by stopped and looked at Amy with some alarm. She asked,

"Are you all right? You look very red in the face. There is an ambulance parked over there in the park, if you need a health check."

"Thank you for your concern. It's some time since I rode a bicycle. Perhaps I will do as you suggest," said Amy.

"Is that your friend riding ahead at speed?" enquired the lady.

"Yes, it is," said Amy.

"Ring your bicycle bell to attract her attention. Let me help you off your bicycle," remarked the lady.

As Amy dismounted from her bicycle with the help of the lady she became very dizzy and fainted. The concerned lady put Amy in the recovery position and went over to the ambulance for assistance. Two paramedics carrying a first-aid bag rushed across to Amy. Jenny looked back and saw the commotion. She cycled back to where Amy lay.

"Are you her friend?" asked one of the paramedics.

"Yes, I am," replied Jenny. "What's the matter with my friend Amy?"

One of the paramedics remarked, "Thanks to the prompt action of this lady your friend has been saved from having the onset of a minor heart attack."

"You're joking," said Jenny.

"No, we are not," replied the paramedic. "Your friend needs to go to hospital right now for a further check-up. I suggest you leave the bicycles and come with us in the ambulance," said one of the paramedics.

Three hours later Amy was discharged from accident and emergency. Jenny, still stunned from the incident, helped Amy into a taxi. They rode back to the hotel in total silence. Jenny paid the taxi driver and assisted Amy up the hotel steps.

"Look, Amy, I'm really sorry about what happened back there in the park. I never imagined it was anything serious."

"If you don't mind I will go up to my room and rest. I'm sure I'll feel fine after a short sleep," said Amy.

"We'll eat at the hotel tonight, Amy," said Jenny. "I'll call for you at seven."

Amy felt better after her sleep. She decided not to take the medication that the hospital had prescribed, as she wanted to enjoy a glass of wine with her meal to celebrate her birthday. Jenny and Amy enjoyed a light evening meal and just one glass of wine.

"I'll see you for breakfast at nine. Have a good night's

sleep, Jenny, and don't worry about me. I'll be OK for tomorrow."

The next morning, after breakfast, Jenny and Amy took the Underground to Westminster Bridge. Jenny bought two tickets for the London Dungeon – another birthday surprise experience for Amy.

"Are you sure you're going to be OK to do this tour?" enquired Jenny.

"Yes, of course I am," said Amy.

They had only just entered the main entrance when Amy clung on to Jenny's arm.

"The tour hasn't started yet, Amy."

"Sorry, Jenny, I've just seen those mice running inside that glass case. I've got a phobia of rats and mice," replied Amy.

"You didn't say," remarked Jenny.

"I'll be OK. Don't worry, Jenny."

The tour was very realistic in parts – particularly the scary boat ride, the plague doctor, Sweeney Todd, Jack the Ripper and the torturer. Amy continued to cling on to Jenny's arm throughout the tour. Amy decided to give the last part of the tour – which was the drop dead ride – a miss. Jenny went on to that ride alone. Amy went through to the shop area to wait for Jenny.

"Wow! That was great. You really felt you were dropping down into a very deep chasm," exclaimed Jenny, as she caught up with Amy in the shop.

"Glad I missed it," said Amy.

"Are you feeling all right, Amy?" asked Jenny.

"Why?" replied Amy.

"No reason, Amy. You look as white as a sheet. I think we had better go and have a hot drink in the cafe before we go on our Thames boat trip," said Jenny.

Amy was relieved to sit down in the cafe. She had felt scared stiff throughout the entire London Dungeon experience. Amy didn't want Jenny to think she was a wimp. The boat trip along the Thames to Greenwich and back was far more relaxing.

Amy and Jenny decided it was time to return to the hotel to freshen up and change for their theatre visit to see Agatha Christie's play *The Mousetrap*... a perfect end to Amy's birthday weekend.

Jenny and Amy enjoyed the play at St Martin's Theatre immensely. They found a bistro nearby and managed to grab a bite to eat before making their way back to their hotel.

"Thanks for a great evening, Jenny – and for a lovely birthday weekend, despite my funny turn in the park," said Amy.

"I'm glad you enjoyed it, Amy, for tomorrow is your last day," exclaimed Jenny. "Sleep well. Oh, and don't forget to take three of the tablets the hospital prescribed tonight, as you've missed your day's dosage because we were out," remarked Jenny.

"That's a good idea, Jenny. I'll do as you suggest. See you tomorrow morning for breakfast at nine."

Before Amy got into bed she took three tablets, as Jenny had advised, with a glass of water. After an hour's sleep Amy woke up with a start. Where on earth was she? The room was spinning round. She felt confused, disoriented and dizzy. Amy was struggling to remember what time Jenny had said for breakfast the next day.

She picked up her mobile phone, but couldn't remember her PIN to unlock it.

This is awful, she thought. *It must be the tablets. Perhaps I shouldn't have taken them all at once... Is Jenny trying to kill me? She did appear to enjoy my feeling fearful in the London Dungeon. Maybe the bike ride in Hyde Park was another attempt by Jenny to kill me off. Why would Jenny behave in such a way?*

All these awful thoughts kept going through Amy's head. She couldn't sleep. What had her mother said to her once about bad luck, and unlucky events happening in threes?

Amy got out of bed and tried to open the door of her room. It wouldn't open. She panicked. This was a living nightmare. She must be hallucinating. Those tablets must be extremely strong. Amy felt her way along the wall of her room and got back into bed. She finally drifted off into a very deep sleep.

The next morning Jenny went to knock on the door of Amy's room to call her for breakfast. There was no reply. Jenny knocked again, and said,

"Are you awake, Amy? It's me, Jenny." There was still no reply. Jenny was beginning to feel rather anxious. Amy must have overslept. She would go down to breakfast anyway. Amy would probably join her later.

An hour passed. The waitress at breakfast had asked Jenny twice if anyone was joining her. Jenny replied, "I'm expecting my friend Amy to join me. She must have overslept. I'll give her ten more minutes, and then I'll call her on my mobile phone."

Ten minutes passed, and Amy had not arrived for breakfast. Jenny rang Amy's mobile number. There was no reply.

Jenny left the breakfast table and made her way over to reception.

"Good morning. I have been expecting my friend in Room 101 to join me for breakfast. She hasn't shown up yet, and an hour has passed. I've called her on my mobile and also knocked on her door, and still there is no reply. I wonder could someone open her room to see if she is OK," requested Jenny.

"Yes. If you would care to accompany the housekeeper she will open your friend's door in your presence," said the receptionist.

Jenny and the housekeeper made their way up to the first floor in the hotel lift. The housekeeper got out her master key and opened Amy's door. The room was in total darkness. The housekeeper opened the curtains. Jenny saw that Amy was lying very still in bed. The housekeeper went over to the bed and gently shook Amy. There was no response.

"Is she breathing?" asked Jenny.

"She doesn't appear to be," replied the housekeeper, who promptly rang down to reception. "The guest in Room 101 isn't waking. I think she may have stopped breathing. Please call a doctor at once."

Jenny was beside herself with worry. The doctor had

been called, and he was still up in Amy's hotel room. Jenny had been asked to wait in the hotel lounge.

Jenny noticed two police officers going up in the hotel lift. She went over to the reception desk.

"Is anything wrong?" enquired Jenny. "I noticed two police officers going up in the lift just now. Are they going to my friend's room?"

"Please go back to the lounge, madam," requested the receptionist. "Someone will be along to take you somewhere more private very shortly to explain what is happening." Jenny went back to the lounge and sat down, but she couldn't settle.

Ten minutes later a tall thin distinguished gentleman in his early forties asked Jenny to follow him into an office just off the main reception. He introduced himself as Peter Morgan, the hotel manager.

"I'm sorry to have to inform you that your friend in Room 101 is dead. The police wish to interview you shortly. Can I bring you a cup of tea or coffee?"

"Did you say my friend was dead? I can't believe it. We were having such a wonderful weekend in London. No, thank you, I don't want a drink," replied Jenny.

The police gave Jenny a thorough grilling about the sequence of events leading up to the death of her friend. They were particularly interested in the advice Jenny had given Amy in relation to taking three tablets together before she went to bed the night before. They asked Jenny if Amy had any history of heart problems, or an allergy to penicillin. Jenny said she was unaware of any such issues, as her friend had always been in good health. The two police officers asked Jenny to accompany them to the police station, where she would be requested to make and sign a formal statement.

Jenny was taken into a small interview room. She was introduced to Detective Inspector Jane Wright. A female police officer stood in the room by the door. DI Wright remarked,

"The doctor has confirmed that your friend died of an overdose of the medication prescribed by the hospital following your cycle ride in Hyde Park. Is there anything further you wish to tell me about this event?"

Jenny was stunned by what she heard.

"I feel absolutely awful about what has happened to my friend. I didn't realise she was struggling to cycle in the park. I wouldn't have persisted with the bicycle ride if I had known Amy wasn't well. As for the overdose of medication… I did advise Amy to take the day's tablets together before she went to sleep as she had missed her daily dosage throughout the day, because we were out."

"Do you have any specific medical knowledge to base your advice on?" asked DI Wright.

"No, I don't," replied Jenny.

This was sounding very serious. DI Wright asked Jenny to remain in the room with the police officer while she went out to have a word with another colleague.

Twenty minutes later DI Wright returned.

"We are going to have to ask you to remain in London for the rest of today. I am sure the hotel will allow you to stay there for a further night. You may wish to call your family to let them know what has happened. Amy's parents are making their way down by train today."

Jenny returned to the hotel. She went up to her room and packed her suitcase. Jenny didn't want to spend another day in London after what had happened. Why were the police asking her to stay another night? Was she going to be charged with the murder of her friend? Jenny couldn't face seeing Amy's parents.

Jenny telephoned her parents to tell them what had happened. They caught the next available train down to London. When they arrived at Jenny's hotel Jenny had checked out of her room and was sitting in the hotel lounge.

"Oh, thank goodness you are both here," said Jenny. "I can't bear to stay here, where Amy died."

"That's OK, sweetheart. We will all check into another hotel near the police station. We'll let the police know where we are staying tonight," said Jenny's father.

"I'm really scared that I'm going to be charged with Amy's murder," sobbed Jenny.

"Don't worry, love. Your father will get a top lawyer to defend you if needs be," said Jenny's mother.

Jenny and her parents went to the police station the next afternoon to meet with Detective Inspector Wright. She informed them all that Jenny was free to leave London. The report by the coroner reached the conclusion, from the evidence presented, that Amy's death was caused by misadventure. Jenny clearly hadn't intended to harm Amy in any way. The cycling incident in Hyde Park and the prescription drug overdose were both unfortunate accidents. Neither Jenny nor Amy knew that she had a weak heart, nor that she was allergic to penicillin. By the time the morning had arrived it was too late to administer an antidote to Amy to counteract the adverse penicillin reaction because she had already died in the night, alone.

Jenny had absolutely nothing to reproach herself for. That was most certainly a birthday surprise to remember.

A RECIPE FOR MURDER

J ustin Thyme, the show host and presenter, greeted the television live audience and said, "Good afternoon, ladies and gentlemen. Welcome to this week's episode of *TV Chefs' Challenge*. In the studio this afternoon our two top TV chefs, Paul Curry and Tony Cook, will battle it out to see which of them can produce the tastiest and most attractive main course using exactly the same ingredients."

Paul Curry and Tony Cook were greeted with enthusiastic applause from the live television audience as they entered the studio. They promptly took up their allotted places at the cooking area, which faced the audience. Paul, as usual, had his mother's favourite recipe book, which he placed on the kitchen worktop in front of him.

"Ah, I see you are hoping to get some inspiration, Paul, from your mother's recipe book," remarked Justin Thyme.

"Yes. I am hoping that one of my mother's signature dishes in her recipe book will give me the leading edge over Tony today," replied Paul jokingly.

"As usual, Paul, you are showing your competitive streak in front of Tony and the studio audience. Let the cooking commence, and may the best chef win."

Wonderful aromas began to hit the television studio audience from the chefs' cooking... fried onions, red wine and garlic, to name but a few. Justin Thyme's stomach began to rumble as he continued his endless running commentary on what each chef was preparing and cooking. Paul had decided to make a posh pasta dish with a wonderful, rich bolognaise sauce. Tony had chosen to create a stir-fry dish, which would be served with a salad or rice. On this occasion Paul hadn't needed to refer to his mother's recipe book for inspiration.

Tony Cook appeared to be far more reticent throughout the afternoon. He gave short, abrupt replies to Justin's inconsequential questions.

What a prize prat Justin really is, thought Tony. *It's bad enough having to produce yet another winning dish in the allotted time without having to listen to his endless pathetic comments and jokes. As for that arrogant smart-arse chef Paul Curry, with his mother's recipe book... well! You could wonder how such a trashy TV show keeps its weekly ratings and its audiences enthralled.*

The atmosphere in the studio kitchen was very hot under the lights. Paul Curry looked flustered. Tony Cook appeared cool and calm, as ever. With only five minutes left the pressure was on. Both chefs began to put the finishing touches to their main courses. The audience counted down.

"Ten, nine, eight, seven, six, five, four, three, two, one... "

"Stop cooking," announced Justin Thyme. Two

members of the audience, picked at random by Justin Thyme, were invited up to judge the chefs' final dishes. Paul's main course was the first to be judged and commented upon for its taste and overall appearance. He was awarded a score of seven out of ten.

Tony's main course, after much praise from the two studio audience judges, was awarded nine out of ten. The two chefs shook hands. Justin Thyme brought the show to a close, and the studio audience left.

Paul and Tony said their goodbyes to each other as they made their way to their cars. Paul unlocked his Porsche Boxster and placed his mother's recipe book on the front passenger seat. Paul reflected for a moment. Perhaps he would have won today's competition if he had based his main course on one of his mother's favourite tried-and-tested recipes. Who knows? For once in his life, though, he had wanted to use his own creative ideas rather than rely on his mother's culinary delights.

Paul started up the car. He looked across at his mother's recipe book on the front seat. Perhaps the best thing he could do would be to get rid of his mother's recipe book once and for all.

He lowered the passenger door window at the front of the car. As he was about to fling his mother's recipe book out of the car window he thought he would take one last look at his mother's written dedication to him on the title page. As he opened the recipe book an almighty explosion occurred within the car. Paul's face and hands were badly damaged in the blast. The smell of burning flesh was nauseating.

The roof of the car had blown off in the explosion. Flames were beginning to engulf Paul.

Before Paul lost total consciousness he could hear the sound of police, ambulance and fire engine sirens in the distance. His career as a top TV chef was well and truly over. That rat Tony Cook must have planned this explosion out of jealousy.

Paul was taken to hospital for emergency treatment. Once the car fire had been extinguished what was left of Paul's car was towed away by a police breakdown truck for further examination.

The local news on television that evening reported the incident. Whether Paul would survive or not was touch-and-go. Tony Cook and Justin Thyme had contacted the hospital to ask how Paul was progressing. Both were genuinely shocked and concerned about Paul. They both hoped that Paul would pull through the trauma.

Justin and Tony couldn't imagine who on earth had done such an awful thing to Paul. The *TV Chefs' Challenge* show would not be the same without him. The serious injuries Paul had sustained would preclude him from participating in the show ever again.

The *Southside Chronicle* reported the next day that the explosion in Paul's car was the result of a tiny explosive device hidden within the centre of a recipe book, the remains of which were found in the front of the car.

It appeared that, on opening the recipe book, Paul had triggered the detonator.

A week later it was revealed that Paul's mother had commissioned an ex-army explosives expert to rig up the device in the recipe book Paul so highly valued. Her motive for the crime was, quite simply, revenge. She was sick and tired of her son Paul trading on her creative cooking skills to further his own career.

BICYCLE FOR SALE

Joe turned to the 'For Sale' section at the back of the local newspaper. One advertisement in particular interested him.

FOR SALE. Gorgeous blue ladies' bicycle: 20-inch frame, 18 gears, 26-inch wheels. Wicker basket at the front. Like new. Unable to ride bicycle due to a recent back injury: £100 cash o.n.o.

The bicycle was just what Joe was looking for. His wife Sue would relish getting back in the saddle again as part of her fitness regime.

Joe telephoned the seller. He arranged to view the bicycle that afternoon at two o'clock.

Joe parked the car outside 22 Beech Road. He walked up the path and rang the doorbell. The door opened slightly, and a woman's voice enquired, "Hello, are you the gentleman who rang up earlier today about viewing the bicycle for sale?"

"Yes, I am." Joe could hear the door chain being released. Standing before him was a tall and elegant smartly dressed lady of middle age with long dark hair. She was wearing a collar to support her neck. Joe presumed this may be as a result of the back injury.

"I'm Jean Frost. I'll take you to the garage to view the bicycle. Follow me." Joe thought she bore a resemblance to Sue from the back.

The bicycle appeared to be in very good condition. Joe took the bicycle for a short ride up and down the road. The brakes worked, the tyres looked fine and the gears changed smoothly.

"Yes, I would like to buy the bicycle and take it away with me today," said Joe. Joe gave Jean Frost the £100 cash. He put the bicycle in the back of his Volvo estate car and waved goodbye.

That night when Sue got in from work Joe took her immediately to the garage.

"Close your eyes, Sue. I've got a surprise for you," remarked Joe.

"Oh, no. Not another one of your DIY projects, Joe."

"No. Much better than that. Now open your eyes, Sue."

Sue let out a gasp of delight when she saw the gorgeous blue bicycle.

"Oh, Joe. Is that for me? It's wonderful. Thank you. I can't wait to go for a ride on it once I've got some cycling gear."

When Sue was equipped she went for a daily forty-minute cycle ride along the country lanes near her home.

One evening, when Sue was taking her usual cycle ride down Green Lane, a silver Ford Focus came up from behind her. It clipped the side of her bicycle, causing her to fall off into the road. She failed to catch sight of the driver or of the car registration number. After getting up from the road she reached for her mobile phone and rang Joe.

"Hi, Joe... nothing to worry about. I've fallen off the bicycle... nothing broken. A car came too close to me. Any chance you could come and collect me and the bike, and take me home in the car?"

"Are you sure you are not hurt?" enquired Joe.

"I'm OK. I didn't see the driver – or get the number of the car, unfortunately," said Sue.

Once Joe got Sue and the bicycle safely back home he made her a cup of tea.

Sue agreed with Joe that it was probably wise, in the circumstances, to stop riding the bicycle at present. Joe decided to contact Jean Frost to find out whether her back injury was the result of a similar cycling incident.

The next day Joe rang Jean Frost's telephone number several times but got no reply. He also went round to her house but, again, got no answer when he rang the doorbell. Joe began to feel rather uneasy. The blue bicycle appeared to be a bad omen.

When Sue returned from work Joe decided they should go out for a pub meal. The pub was fairly quiet, with just a few customers drinking at the bar. They ordered their food and drinks. The meal was good, and Sue began to relax. As Sue and Joe left the pub they noticed a short blonde-haired middle-aged stocky bloke leaving just ahead of them. Unbelievably, he got into a silver Ford Focus. Sue was certain that this was the car that had knocked her off her bike, as it had a dent in the front bumper on the nearside.

"Joe, I think that the car that is starting up over there is the one that knocked me off my bike."

"Right," said Joe. "Get in the car quickly, and I will follow it."

Joe and Sue gave chase in their Volvo estate. Joe put his foot hard down on the car's accelerator pedal. He moved the Volvo quickly across from the inside lane over to the outside lane, only narrowly missing another car on the dual carriageway. Joe proceeded at high speed to tailgate the silver Ford Focus in front of him all the way up to the end of the dual carriageway.

Sue was speechless. She felt terrified. She couldn't believe how dangerously Joe was driving. He was like a man possessed... so out of character. Sue just wanted Joe to slow down and get them home safely, in one piece. As they approached the roundabout at the end of the dual carriageway the silver Ford Focus pulled away suddenly, and travelled onwards in the opposite direction.

Joe cursed, "Damn and blast, he's got away from us."

When Joe and Sue eventually arrived home Sue felt so shaken. Joe got out of the Volvo and slammed the driver's door shut in his anger. Sue slowly began to remove her seat belt. She couldn't move. Joe rushed over to Sue's passenger door and helped her out of the car. Sue's legs felt like jelly as she closed the car door.

Joe began to apologise to Sue and said, "I'm so sorry for compromising your safety by driving like a bat out of hell."

"That was terrifying, Joe. It was a white-knuckle ride. A journey to thrill or kill. Either way… don't ever drive like that again, Joe."

"I was only trying to get the driver in the silver Ford Focus to stop," replied Joe.

"Life's too short, Joe," Sue said sadly, as she made her way into the house.

She went straight to bed.

Joe made his decision. He telephoned the police to report all the events leading up to the car chase that evening. The police requested Joe to report to the police station the next morning. In the meantime they agreed to trace the owner of the silver Ford Focus, as Joe had remembered the registration number.

In the morning, after dropping Sue off at work, Joe drove on to the police station. The police officer invited Joe through to the back office. Joe sat down at the desk. The police officer joined him and opened a folder.

"Yes, the driver of the silver Ford Focus is already known to the police. You did the right thing in telling us about the bicycle incident, about the lack of reply from Jean Frost and about your car chase last night. The driver, Brian Frost, has now been arrested on suspicion of murdering his wife, Jean Frost."

Joe was shocked by what he had just heard. The police officer continued, "Brian Frost admitted that he thought your wife looked like his wife from the back when riding the blue bicycle the other day. That is why he drove into her."

Joe, after signing his witness statement, left the police station and drove back home.

He then telephoned the local newspaper to place an advertisement in the 'For Sale' section, as he wished to sell a ladies' gorgeous blue bicycle.

WRITERS' CIRCLE

Beth Watson, recently retired primary school teacher, looked at her bucket list. She had set herself three goals for the year:

Join a local writing group.

Learn to paint with watercolours.

Go on a short cruise.

Charlie Roberts – owner of BOOKCASE, the local bookshop – had persuaded Beth to join Writers' Circle, the local writing group. This new writing group met every Monday evening at his bookshop. As Charlie lived in the same road as Beth he was able to give her a lift in his car each Monday. Beth's secret desire was to write and publish a book of short stories. Beth hoped that Writers' Circle would help her to fulfil her burning ambition.

Charlie, a retired university senior lecturer in English, had bought and opened BOOKCASE with his redundancy money two years ago. He hadn't made a fortune from the bookshop, but he had made his bachelor life far more interesting. Beth didn't know what to expect in terms of how experienced and skilled the other members of the Writers' Circle were. Charlie had reassured her that she would fit in very well.

The doorbell rang. Beth grabbed her coat and

bag and opened the door. Charlie greeted her and led her to his car. Beth got in the car and fastened her seat belt. While they were driving along Beth asked Charlie about the members of Writers' Circle. Charlie said, "There are two other members besides me. Pete is an accountant in his mid-twenties who's single, and a bit of a ladies' man. He hopes to write a crime novel. Liz is a school secretary in her early forties. She is married with two children in their late teens. Liz enjoys writing poetry, and at present hasn't any ambitions to publish."

"I look forward to meeting them this evening, Charlie, and perhaps hearing them read some of their creative offerings," replied Beth.

On arrival at BOOKCASE Charlie helped Beth out of the car. He unlocked the bookshop door, put on the lights and plugged in the electric heater. Beth hung her coat up. Charlie had put the kettle on to boil to make a hot drink when the other members of Writers' Circle arrived. Beth helped Charlie arrange four chairs round the table at the back of the bookshop. Just then the bookshop door opened, and in walked Pete and Liz.

"What a night," exclaimed Pete as he took off his coat. "It's just begun to rain."

"Well, hello, Liz. Fancy seeing you here. I didn't know you were a secret writer. Mind you, you must relish writing something far more creative when faced with typing the school newsletter and letters to parents," remarked Beth.

"Oh, do you two know each other?" replied Charlie.

"Yes, we do," said Liz. "I'm a secretary in the office at the primary school that Beth has just retired from."

"What a coincidence," remarked Charlie. "It's certainly a small world."

Pete gave a half smile at Beth and didn't say anything. Everyone helped themselves to a hot drink and sat down around the table. Charlie welcomed Beth formally to Writers' Circle, and commented on the fact that she would make a valuable contribution to the writers' group.

Beth enjoyed the first session of Writers' Circle, especially listening to the others read out their latest piece of writing. Beth appreciated the lift home in Charlie's car, especially as the rain was much heavier now. Beth said to Charlie,

"I thought Pete was rather reticent, and not very welcoming in having a new member join Writers' Circle."

"I wouldn't let Pete put you off. He can be a bit moody at times. I suppose that being an accountant and working with figures all day makes him appear aloof," remarked Charlie. On reaching home Beth thanked Charlie for the lift. Charlie asked Beth, "Would you like to go to the theatre one night with me?" She thanked him for his kind offer and added, "I'm rather busy over the next few weeks, catching up with friends who I haven't seen for a while. Perhaps another time, Charlie."

The next morning, when Beth went to pick up the post from the hall carpet, she came across a letter among the usual pile of junk mail and utility bills. It was postmarked from a neighbouring town. Intrigued, Beth opened the envelope and took out the letter. To her horror, there was a short message, which had been produced from printed cut-out letters and stuck on to the writing paper. The message read:

HOW DOES IT FEEL TO KNOW YOU HUMILIATED SOMEONE AND MADE THEIR LIFE HELL?

Who could have sent such an unpleasant letter? thought Beth. Her immediate reaction was to throw the letter away. On reflection she decided not to be so hasty, and put the letter in the hall table drawer. Beth found it hard to concentrate for the remainder of the day and night. She couldn't settle. It was probably best just to ignore the poison pen letter. For that was what it was.

Beth tried to think if she had upset anyone recently. The only new people in her life at present were the three members of Writers' Circle. She couldn't imagine any of them doing such a despicable thing. Beth decided not to discuss the poison pen letter with anyone.

Best to move on and forget it, she thought.

Another week passed, and a second poison pen letter arrived through the post. Beth was dreading opening it. What insulting, hurtful things would it say this time?

The tone of the letter was far more threatening, spiteful and malicious. It said:

YOU DON'T DESERVE TO ENJOY
A HAPPY RETIREMENT, YOU BITCH.
MAY YOU BURN.

Beth's mind went into overdrive. Perhaps it was sent from someone in the Writers' Circle. After all, she was the new girl. Perhaps she had been a bit rude to all three of them during the first session. She had been a bit patronising towards Liz when she had queried how she could possibly write creatively when all she did at work was churn out school newsletters and letters to parents.

She had let Charlie down and disappointed him by not accepting his invitation to go to the theatre. Perhaps this rejection had fired up his revenge.

Then there was Pete. He didn't appear to like her very much at all. This was evident from his behaviour towards her in the writing sessions. He never talked to her, looked at her or showed any interest in her work.

Beth felt frightened. If her gut reactions were making her feel uneasy about her colleagues in Writers' Circle then she couldn't confide in them, or discuss the poison pen letters with any of them.

Beth put the letter back in the envelope and slipped it into the hall table drawer. Once again, Beth found it hard to settle to anything for the rest of the day. That night she tossed and turned in bed as she struggled to get to sleep.

Three days later a third poison pen letter landed on the hall carpet with the other post. Beth opened this letter first. It said:

HOPE I'VE PRICKED YOUR CONSCIENCE.
MAY YOU SUFFER A LONG, LINGERING
PAINFUL DEATH.
FAREWELL, YOU BITCH.

Enough was enough. Beth put the letter back in its envelope. She took out the other two poison pen letters from the hall table drawer. Beth telephoned the police to report the incident. A female police officer called later that afternoon to view the letters. She asked Beth if she had any suspicions as to who may be sending the letters, or the motive behind such an action. Beth was unable to shed any light on the situation. The police officer put the letters in a clear plastic evidence bag and took them back to the police station for forensic examination.

Beth didn't hear anything further from the police for two days. Beth had rung Charlie at BOOKCASE up the following Monday morning to inform him that she wasn't feeling very well, and that she wouldn't be going to Writers' Circle that evening.

"I do hope you will feel better soon, as we will all miss your input tonight," said Charlie.

The following morning Beth received a phone call from the police. Detective Inspector Dan Neal wished to visit her at home, after lunch. When the doorbell rang Beth rushed to open the door. After DI Dan Neal showed Beth his ID she led him through to the lounge. He began to update Beth on the progress the police had made with their enquiries. The backgrounds of all members of Writers' Circle, including her own, had been investigated. Pete Maloney was the chief suspect. His old primary school records indicated that he was frequently in trouble as a result of his disruptive classroom behaviour. Beth realised that Pete had been a pupil at the school, where she had previously taught, and had actually been in her class in Years 5 and 6.

DI Dan Neal went on to relate that Pete Maloney, after moving on to his secondary school, had been found to be dyslexic. This accounted for why he masked his literacy learning difficulties with bad behaviour at primary school. He didn't want to lose his credibility in front of his other classmates. Beth, according to Pete Maloney, had put him down and humiliated him in front of his peers. This had lowered his confidence and self-esteem. He could never forgive Beth for the way she had treated him in her class.

Pete had admitted to the police that he had sent the poison pen letters to Beth. His pent-up frustrations over the years had resulted in Pete bearing a grudge against Beth. Her joining the Writers' Circle gave him the perfect opportunity to seek revenge.

Under Section One of the Malicious Communications Act 1988 Pete was convicted of the offence of sending grossly offensive, threatening poison pen letters to Beth Watson with the intent to frighten, insult and upset her. Beth's reputation and personal safety had been compromised. Even though she may have made Pete feel inadequate in her class she was not to blame for Pete's persecution complex. Pete was fined £1,000 by the magistrate.

Pete, for obvious reasons, never returned to the Writers' Circle at BOOKCASE.

Three new members joined the writing group. Beth eventually returned to the Writers' Circle, when her guilty feelings left her. She agreed to go out with Charlie to the theatre, and for a meal. He had shown genuine concern for her in her absence from the writing group, as had Liz.

BURNING DESIRE

Harry Green, the local estate agent, was delighted to have found a mug – or, rather, a buyer – for the empty, ramshackle house that had been on his books for just over two years. The house itself was in a very poor state of repair externally.

The interior was a shell, which required total redecoration and refurbishment throughout. The one-acre garden was dreadfully overgrown. Three of the neighbours had constantly complained to the local council about the plague of rats that was invading their immaculate gardens from the overgrown jungle.

The young couple who had bought the house, James and Lynne Cooper, were desperate to own their first home. Lynne had great plans for the renovation of the house. She dreamt about creating the ideal home, where James and she could raise a family while enjoying the good life in suburbia. It was a huge project for James and Lynne Cooper to manage. However, as they had got the house at a knock-down bargain price (according to the estate agent), this meant that they had a larger budget available for upgrading the house and garden.

James decided that Lynne and he would live in a camper van in the rear garden while the house renovations took place. The essential external house repairs would be done first. Then the Coopers would work on creating their master bedroom, and installing a new bathroom and kitchen. Once this work was completed James and Lynne could move out of the camper van and live in the house. The redecoration and upgrading of the other rooms would follow.

The overgrown jungle of a garden posed the greatest challenge to the Coopers. Neither of them knew the first thing about gardening, having moved from a city apartment with only a window box. Perhaps their immediate neighbours would be able to recommend a reputable local landscape gardening firm who could work miracles in creating a natural green haven. James and Lynne were yet to meet their neighbours. They knew very little about the neighbourhood, other than it was a respectable district in which to live and eventually rear a family. Lynne and James felt it was probably wiser to wait until they had created a habitable home before inviting the neighbours round for drinks.

The Coopers' camper van was barely visible in the overgrown back garden. The trees – or, rather, the forest – that towered way above the roof of the house provided a good level of cover and privacy for James and Lynne. The neighbours were unaware that James and Lynne Cooper were actually living on the premises.

Nigel Parkinson, leader of the local neighbourhood campaign group 'Save Our Environment', worked tirelessly with other residents to keep their locality clean, tidy and pleasant. He was becoming extremely irritated by the local eyesore of the empty boarded-up dilapidated house with its overgrown garden. Both were creating a blot on the local landscape. The council never succeeded in keeping the plague of canny rats, which tunnelled their way under the neighbouring garden fences from the wilderness of the neglected garden, at bay.

The other residents in the local campaign group actually knew very little about their leader. He didn't appear to have a nine-to-five job like the rest of them. They assumed that he worked from home because of the large shed in his garden, part of which had been converted into an office. Men in sheds were something of a rarity in Millionaires' Row.

Nigel Parkinson was like a dog with a bone. He wouldn't give up a fight easily. His short temper and low tolerance level clearly indicated that he didn't suffer fools gladly. This accounted for why the other local residents were quite happy for Nigel to take the council to task over the empty, ramshackle house with its overgrown garden.

"Your sins and mine will be redeemed very shortly, for I have the burning desire to get to the bottom of the empty house and garden jungle once and for all," said Nigel, as he addressed the meeting of the local 'Save Our Environment' campaign group.

"I would avoid taking the law into your own hands, Nigel," remarked one of the residents.

"Don't worry. I'm sure it won't come to that, because I've got the support of our local Member of Parliament to fight the cause. She will certainly get things moving with the local council," replied Nigel.

James and Lynne poured themselves another glass of rosé as they studied the house renovation plans for the last time before going to bed. Lynne went to open the camper van door to allow some fresh air to enter. She thought she could detect a petrol-like smell. She went to check if the camper van's petrol cap was secure. It was. Lynne went back into the camper van and closed the door. James and Lynne retired to bed for the night.

Lynne woke up suddenly in the night. It was extremely hot in the camper van. She thought she could smell smoke. She nudged James awake from his sleep.

"Hey, James. It's really hot in the camper van, and I can smell smoke." James got up. He went over to the camper van door. James grabbed the handle of the door but withdrew his hand instantly, as it was far too hot to hold. The door wouldn't open. James moved over to the camper van's side window but, alas, that also failed to open.

James looked outside the window of the camper van. He saw flames leaping and dancing around the camper van. He grabbed Lynne's hand.

"Our camper van is engulfed in flames. We must try to get out of here before the petrol tank on the van explodes," said James.

Too late. At that very moment an almighty explosion occurred. James and Lynne were thrown across the camper van floor. The camper van was filling up quickly with filthy, dense black smoke. The interior of the van was now ablaze. James held Lynne tightly in his arms. They couldn't breathe.

James and Lynne lost consciousness.

It took the fire brigade several hours to contain the blaze, which had spread to the empty house. There was nothing left but a smouldering, black heap of detritus.

The entire event was devastating for the residents, as they had to be evacuated from their homes. It seemed to take weeks to get the smell of smoke out of their houses. What was even more traumatic was the discovery of a burnt-out camper van with the charred remains of two human beings at the bottom of the burnt-out garden. Dental records had identified the human remains as belonging to James and Lynne Cooper, the new owners of the empty property.

Nigel Parkinson had disappeared shortly after the incident. Police arrested him at a nearby garage as he was refuelling his car on the forecourt. His trial took place shortly afterwards at the Crown Court. The judge convicted him of first-degree arson, as he had committed a criminal act by deliberately setting fire to the grounds. He was given a life sentence in prison by the judge.

It turned out that Nigel Parkinson was a pyrotechnician who specialised in organising large-scale firework displays for commercial and leisure organisations. He had extensive expertise in the origin, nature and control of fires, as well as knowing how to handle explosives. By committing arson Nigel Parkinson had not only put the lives of the other residents at risk but he had also murdered the Coopers. He had endeavoured to plead his innocence at the trial in relation to the Coopers, and emphasised that he didn't know they were living in a camper van on the premises.

Nigel Parkinson's burning desire was an extremely high price to pay just for sorting out a plague of rats.

ABOUT THE AUTHOR

R ita Cheminais is the author of twenty previous best-selling academic books on special educational needs. *Twelve Thrilling Tales* is her very first fiction collection of short stories in the crime and thriller genre.

In her spare time Rita is a film and TV extra, a promotional model and a commercial voice-over artist. She is a member of the Liverpool Rotunda Writers. Rita lives in Crosby, Merseyside.